A Tale of Three Women

Also by the Author

Searching for Ambergris

The Nights, The Days

The Shortest Distance

Time & Distance

A Tale of Three Women

A Novella
by
Kathleen Thompson

Kathleen Thompson

Excalibur Press 2020
Daphne, Alabama

A Tale of Three Women

Published in the United States of America
by
Excalibur Press
P. O. Box 2929
Daphne, Alabama 36526
Excaliburpress@msn.com
www.excaliburpress.us

Cover art by James Elwood Slowe
Cover design by Nicholas Vincent Renda, Jr.
Rear cover Author Photo by Angie Holder

Printed in the United States of America
First Edition, 2020
ISBN 978-0-9820629-6-8

Dedication

*T*o Sena Jeter Naslund, Founding Director of the Spalding MFA program, who invited me to row my little fishing boat into the waters of leviathans, and who through her grace and her fiction, has been life-changing for me;

to Mary Clyde, my first fiction mentor at Spalding, who read the short story that birthed this novella and noted that it had "a fable-like quality in that it teaches us something about the human condition...the characters are trying to create themselves." Under Mary's guidance I pushed this story to the limits of its quirkiness as it grew. She allowed a certain *why-ness* in my stories, without requiring their precise *when, where,* and *how.* Those stories were often a kind of initial non-linear fuzziness that in the end drew the story into a pleasing whole. All that semester I found myself wallowing in writing such stories under an adopted and clandestine (except to my mentor) pseudonym, V. Hasseltine Taylor;

to Neela Vaswani, my final fiction mentor at Spalding, who with exuberance and wisdom offered, during the organizing of my thesis stories, "...I must say that reading the two [stories] in succession was very pleasing for me. The one bolsters the other; together, they read like a charming novella...What's sad is the missed opportunity. How life happens in ways we don't expect. That's the tragedy of the story as I see it...";

to the remainder of the fiction faculty and fellow students, 2001-2003, who in multiple ways helped keep my little poetry/fiction boat afloat in Spalding's rising tide;

to the memory of James Duncan (1950-2017) my nephew, yard man, and storyteller who learned much as groundskeeper for Hudson Strode. James knew Strode was a well-known writing teacher at the University of Alabama; Strode also liked to tell stories. He told of the fish fountain—a gift from the King of Sweden, of a visit to Key West, of the cats, and his complaints about Hemingway's loud early morning typing. The colorful stories I was hearing from James's dubious life and the anonymity of a pseudonym, catapulted the reality of my stories up a notch. My epiphany: real life stories could be transformed into riveting fictive tales. "Strode told me that he was going to put me in his book," James asserted. I have searched Strode's *The Eleventh House*, "a book of friends who were collected and cherished by Hudson Strode." But James most likely was edited out for the likes of such famous friends as Ernest Hemingway, or the King of Sweden—or Alabama's own Helen Norris. Not to worry, James, for just as I promised, here's your mention in *my* book. You're not forgotten. You are missed dreadfully;

to M.F., who shared the breakfast duty with me at Hayden Harris, our co-op dorm, as well as a first name and a maiden name. My dear friend has read this story and others of mine, always with honest critique and encouragement. She, along with the two other "Bad News Buddies," Ivodean and Carol, initiated me into the real world in more ways than I should name;

to James Elwood Slowe for his brilliant sculpture which may offer further insights into my little tale;

to Kenny Rogers, for his close reading and insightful critique of the story;

to Nicholas Vincent Renda, Jr. for his breathtaking (spoken like a true Gran) cover design and for his creative eye in all things;

to Linda and Don Parker at Excalibur Press: Without an ending there is no story; without a story there is no book; and without a book there can be no publisher and editor. Without you both, my words and James's might have remained hidden on some hard drive, or rotting away in a file drawer—formless, unattended, of no particular notice at all. I am grateful for its being brought to life.

A Tale of Three Women

Kathleen Thompson

Will what is molded say to the one who molds it,
"Why have you made me like this?"
Has the potter no right over the clay,
to make out of the same lump
one object for special use and another for ordinary use?

-Romans 9:21b-22

Prologue

Long ago and far away in a little village a tale was spun of two women who had little in common except their identical names: Madeira Mae Smith. This idyllic town centered around a mill that used creosote to preserve tall poles that held up telephone wires. The village was called Brownville. Neither J. Graham Brown nor his brother lived in the village, but they owned the wood preserving plant and the people who worked there. J. Graham Brown, no doubt, knew few of the residents as well as he knew Tidy Sum, Bornastar, and Seven Hearts, his favorite horses to regularly bet on at home in Louisville. Creating this village was an investment he hoped would prove more secure than betting on horses, and perhaps half as pleasing to him as his companion and lapdog, Woozems, a white poodle.

A paved road led into the village road and curved off west leading to the commissary and the post office. The Community Center—sitting just off the road at the entrance to the village—was a huge white clapboard structure of two stories which stood in stark contrast to the

1

small, simple homes made of black wood, creosoted for longer life. The building served as a center for both worship and entertainment, and often the two overlapped. For entertainment, unlikely men dressed up as women for womanless weddings. Real weddings were also performed there. Baptists and Methodists alternated Sundays for worship. Baptists could baptize in the swimming hole in nearby Sipsey River, while the Methodists only needed a small basin for sprinkling. On Saturday nights a movie was shown for a dime, usually a rip-roaring Lash LaRue western.

Brownville Elementary School sat near the Community Center, but the enrollment had outgrown the size of the school building, requiring the use of a county school bus to transport the children to Montgomery School a few miles away.

Only the main road was paved; the others were dirt. Some people lived on the hill, some lived on the main road, and some lived below the railroad tracks. Such classic socioeconomic design requires little explanation. Mr. Hodo, the Plant Superintendent, lived on the crest of the hill. Light years below, the Quarters were located close enough to the plant that the smell of black creosote, as pungent as wood pulp cooking, was omnipresent. But the odor seemed as natural to occupants as the sweet smells of a pot of boiling turnip greens or collards.

A Tale of Three Women

The main road was extended below the hill and called Shotgun Town. Those houses were of that design so that if you stood at the front door and fired a gun straight ahead, the bullet would go through the door of each room of the house. Shotgun Town and the sprinkling of houses just beyond the tracks were both areas for those transient whites who did not quite belong on the main road where a few houses had indoor plumbing, and certainly not on the upper road, where some houses had closets, a pantry, and a large claw-footed bathtub. Air conditioners were unheard of except at the superintendent's house, so windows were always open in the summer. In the winter coal heaters placed in the middle of the front room heated the houses. Screened porch doors were never latched unless someone had the opportunity or occasion to be scantily dressed at mid-afternoon.

The village had a tiny office for the company doctor across from the commissary. Next to it was a small post office and if you were old enough and had lived there long enough, you had your own P.O. Box; otherwise, you requested your mail from Postmistress Tyndall. She reluctantly released the infrequent letter out under the bars that covered her little cage. People felt safe in the village, so there were no real reasons for bars. The Wanted mug shots on her small bulletin board, except maybe for one, seemed as unlikely to be a real person as Miss Tyndall, whose posture was so stiff and straight one could not imagine her eating biscuits and gravy for breakfast or sleeping or performing any other bodily functions.

The train tracks ran alongside the commissary. There the plant hands stopped to gas up their trucks, or if they walked to work, to buy a Dr. Pepper or Orange Crush and a bag of Tom's peanuts or a Baby Ruth bar. If the housewife should run out of a staple, say lard, flour, baking powder, baking soda, washing powders, or starch, she sent her child with a pencil-scrawled list to the commissary. The storekeeper would fill her bill and cheerfully add it to the running tally. The child could take the path home behind the commissary, hoping to encounter a frog or a box turtle or a bird's nest with eggs or sometimes even a garden snake in the undergrowth that bordered the path. The ultimate hope was that the train would be going by, and a big wave to its engineer, Mr. Kendrick, would get at least one extra long toot of the train whistle.

On Saturdays some of the more frugal mill hands drove the twenty miles into Northport and shopped at the Yellow Front Store for goods priced half as much as those in the commissary. Few, however, who lived beyond the tracks, had cars or the wherewithal to save money. Indeed, when weekly paychecks were dispensed, the plant hands came by the commissary to cash the checks and to leave most of their money there. If a few coins were left over, one could slip up to the Quarters for a pint of home-brewed libation issued through a back door.

The little black steam engine, No. 97, and Mr. Kendrick made a morning and evening run to and from the creosote plant, pulling in a box car filled with coal, and an empty one out again. The coal was burned to make steam to power the shop activities of the plant. The train's whistle coming in and leaving was as regular as the plant's whistle. On the wood yard, poles were laid in great stacks. Some of the poles were in their natural state, some were peeled and naked, and others had already been creosoted black. Those would be carried to the GM&O junction at Buhl. Crane operators moved the poles from one pile to another as space was required, or as orders for poles were filled, or new loads brought in on logging trucks. The pole yard was separated into the black one which held the creosoted poles and the white pole yard which held the unprocessed poles.

Nothing was left to the imagination in this village. The plant whistle embodied an authority akin to mission bells. The five o'clock whistle woke the people up, the seven o'clock whistle signaled time to stomp out the cigarettes and begin the day, the noon whistle signaled lunch, the one o'clock that lunch had ended, and the four o'clock that the day shift was over and time for the next shift to begin their routine. On New Year's Eve at midnight the men on the graveyard shift blew the whistle for an extended period, grateful for another year of steady employment. They had not heard of the skepticism of scientists on the subject of time and how it might not be flowing at all but static. The times of their lives were marked by the plant's whistle.

It was not the best of times in Brownville, nor was it the worst of times. The village was bound by the Sipsey River on the west, the Community Center on the North, Mr. Hobson, the mail carrier's house on the east, and Mt. Zion Freewill Baptist roughly to the south, and except for the weekly trip to town on Saturday, people stayed within those boundaries. Most summer evenings people spent lounging on the front porch swing, but a few television antennas could be seen on top of the creosoted houses.

People watched Andy Griffith and remarked that they had their own Opie who lived in Shotgun Town. Any obvious differences in Jimmy Clyde's temperament which vacillated between fiery and melancholic, and Opie's, were simply ignored. Some villagers swooned over Rowdy Yates and wept at the tidiness with which he could tame any problems of the wild, wild west, in "Rawhide." And the housewives (which did not include either of the Madeira Maes) lived their lives sprinkling and ironing starched clothes in front of "As the World Turns" or "Guiding Light," waiting for the plant whistle to tell them when their husbands would be home. Not one of them had ever heard of Picasso. Not even Jimmy Clyde.

Part 1

You've Got to Fly

A Tale of Three Women

Jimmy Clyde was mad enough to shit nails. Just because some old man Brown from Kentucky owned this whole damned creosote-soaked town, and just because old man Hodo acted like he owned the whole damned place didn't mean either one of them owned his sorry ass, and Jimmy Clyde was going to tell Hodo so today.

Whittling was just whittling to some people but the end-result for Jimmy Clyde was something more. Just after Mydearie Mae moved to Brownville in third grade, after about a million jumps from the low branch of a small oak, he had finally managed to catch a robin with his hands. He told her he had always thought that cupping that bird within his two hands would improve his whittling, but it was not until he attempted the pterodactyl had he realized it was something more than the holding. Birds were born to fly.

He wasn't sure Mydearie Mae really understood then, in third grade, nor now, in twelfth grade, the difference in capture and freedom. Now she was too eaten up filling out forms for colleges and college loans to even think about his whittling. Maybe nobody could understand.

Unless it was his first-grade teacher, Miss Madeira, not ever to be confused with Mydearie Mae, his girlfriend. Miss Madeira could almost be Mydearie Mae's older sister. Even in Miss Madeira's class, he could already draw squirrels and redbirds by heart for her bulletin boards.

Later he'd stop in afternoons to see if she needed some help cleaning the blackboards. When he was in tenth grade, his mama died with a stroke. That year he also failed his first algebra test and nearly quit school. He decided to visit his old first grade classroom and take Miss Madeira a squirrel he had whittled from cedar. It held an acorn on a cedar base. Jimmy Clyde had not explained the gift—that he had been whittling it for his mama, nor did he tell Miss Madeira he was considering quitting school. "Oh, that little face is so lifelike," she said, turning it to see the details.

Jimmy Clyde smiled, aware of the slight bulge in his pocket from his whittling knife he called the Fightin' Rooster.

The very next afternoon, as Jimmy Clyde was walking past the commissary to see Mydearie Mae, Mr. Hodo called him over to the gas pump. He asked Jimmy Clyde about helping out around the commissary on afternoons and weekends: pumping gas, maybe checking and adding oil to cars.

As it turned out, those two were like ham and eggs. Mr. Hodo had once tried whittling, but was no good at it. Both liked keeping things orderly. Once a task presented itself, Mr. Hodo liked how eager Jimmy Clyde was to get it done. He'd said so more than once. But Jimmy Clyde was not trying to please Mr. Hodo. He simply liked things a certain way. He liked getting the work done and filling the other hours with what he really wanted to do.

When Mr. Hodo saw how Jimmy Clyde busied himself in between jobs by whittling, he was so impressed he purchased some carving knives and some cedar soft enough for Jimmy Clyde to sculpt easily. Then he told Jimmy Clyde he would set him up with the local arts and crafts fairs in town. The superintendent would give him ten per cent of all the profit. Jimmy Clyde wanted nothing to do with being friends with Mr. Hodo, but being in business, well, that suited Jimmy Clyde just fine.

Or it did before Jimmy Clyde's pterodactyl. He had spotted the Honduras mahogany, three board feet, at a carpentry shop in Northport and bought it for five dollars and the promise of eight hours of work cleaning up around the shop. As soon as he touched the mahogany and held it in both hands, his fingers felt the pattern emerging, and as it emerged for the very first time, Jimmy Clyde made a discovery. It was not the catching or holding of that robin in his hands in third grade that he wanted to capture within his whittled pieces: it was the letting go.

So, his pterodactyl was *not* for sale. Not even, by damn, to Hodo. Not his soul and especially not his best piece of work. As soon as this last year of high school was over, he was looking to get a job in Northport. Maybe the wood shop behind Faucett's. It was fine to work here in the commissary on afternoons and Saturdays, but he was not going to peel any poles on the stinking black pole yard. No way in hell....

The pole yard was too close to the smell of creosote and he hated it as bad as Mydearie Mae hated the smell of Evening in Paris. The seven o'clock plant whistle had just shrieked the final summons to Jimmy Clyde's customers. He selected his breakfast Coca-cola from the red chest of ice. He snapped the bottle top off with the opener on the side, chugalugged the small drink in two swallows, and set the bottle into a wooden crate of empties. He marked it down on the little notebook on which he kept his own running tab near the cash register. Then he drew the stool away from the cash register and sat down. He had to stand up again to reach into his jeans pocket for his knife. He picked up the small whetstone that lay on the counter. He held the stone in his left hand and drew the largest blade of his four-blade Fighting Rooster carefully up one side of the whetstone, flipped the blade over, and whisked it down the other side. His mop of red hair peaked at the crown like feathers and moved a little as he developed a steady sharpening rhythm. Behind him on a shelf sat a row of whittled animals, mostly squirrels and birds from cedar. In the middle was his prized mahogany pterodactyl.

Madeira Mae had tried to talk him out of it yesterday. She took a long slow sip of her Dr. Pepper, and then said,

"Jimmy Clyde, don't get that red-headed temper of yours riled up. Let 'im sell it. You can whittle another one."

"Another one ain't the point, Mydearie Mae. This one here's the point. Ain't no two alike. If I whittle now till doomsday, I couldn't get that same wing lift or that big, pointy beak. I don't even have the encyclopedia picture anymore."

Jimmy Clyde lifted the carving off the shelf and held the pterodactyl up to the light. The beam of sunlight from a window had dust motes in it, but the polished mahogany gleamed.

"Ten dollars. Ten measly dollars is the price he wants to ask. Old Man Hodo can just kiss my rusty ass."

***

Mydearie Mae was sitting on the commissary steps waiting for Miss Tyndall. Miss Tyndall had told her yesterday to come back to the post office this morning. A letter from Detroit was addressed to Madeira Mae Smith, but she wasn't sure it belonged to Mydearie Mae.

Mydearie Mae just knew the letter was for her. Jimmy Clyde had promised before he left a few weeks ago. She had already had a lot of long nights to think about whether she would go to Detroit even if Jimmy Clyde kept his promise to mail her a bus ticket. And even though she wasn't exactly sure what she would do, she was sure it was her letter, and certain that she was going to get it this morning, even if she had to snatch it from Miss Tyndall's greedy little hands.

From the very day she first met him, Jimmy Clyde had been doing things that left Mydearie Mae breathless. This time it was far worse than jumping from a tree and trying to catch a robin in flight. For her, "a bird in the hand" meant something entirely different from learning how to whittle. She came from a family of making do and was not one to take chances on anything that could not be pinned down, made secure. Mydearie Mae was a senior in high school and already had been offered a tuition scholarship to the University in the fall. She planned on working at the Supe Store for the summer but had been promised a job at the campus switchboard. It paid ninety cents an hour.

A lone buzzard circled over the side of the commissary near the garbage heap. *One for sorrow...* Madeira Mae strained to see more buzzards, wishing for at least one more to count—*two for joy, three for a letter, four for a boy.* She shaded her eyes and noticed the flag going up. Miss Tyndall had slipped out through the back door. Mydearie Mae walked over to the post office and stood stone still behind Miss Tyndall as she secured the flag to the pole.

Mydearie Mae announced more sharply than she'd intended, "Do you have *my* letter?"

"Oh, you scared me." Miss Tyndall shrugged.

A Tale of Three Women

As Miss Tyndall marched back into the tiny building, she slowly pulled the envelope from her skirt pocket. "I'm sorry. This letter is addressed to the Miss Madeira on Rural Route One. You know her. Madeira Mae Smith. She teaches first grade and lives up on Mormon Road."

She slipped the envelope back into her pocket. "Now, Mydearie Mae, you don't know a soul in Detroit, do you?"

She *did* know someone in Detroit all right, but she wasn't about to tell Miss Tyndall or anyone else. And, of course, she knew Miss Madeira. Everybody at the school knew the first-grade teacher. Mydearie Mae had been teased about having a "teacher name, teacher name" ever since that first roll call when she'd moved there in third grade. Miss Tyndall knew good and well she knew Miss Madeira. Why had Jimmy Clyde been so stupid? He had probably never written a single letter before this.

"I've been writing to colleges all over the country."

"Sorry. Not from a college. This is a personal letter— addressed by hand. I'll send it on out with today's mail. Mr. Hobson will return it if it doesn't belong to her."

"But, it's for me. It's *my* name," Mydearie Mae pleaded. "Let me have it."

"Young lady, this envelope is clearly addressed to Rural Route One." Miss Tyndall was now safely behind the barred window. She pulled down the sliding door behind the bars and held the envelope up for Mydearie

Mae to see. "See here. Go on home now, and ask your mother if she has any collards for sale."

Mydearie Mae's feet felt stuck in concrete, and dried. Miss Tyndall and everybody else around knew good and well her mama didn't sell anything from her garden. Miss Tyndall had the nerve. She was just fishing for free collards. She heard Miss Tyndall close the back door and come around front, but she couldn't move. Miss Tyndall ignored her as she moved notices around on the bulletin board and thumbtacked up a new Wanted poster.

***

First thing when she had arrived that morning, Miss Tyndall mulled over the envelope. In her forty-some years of civil service, Miss Tyndall had experienced up to now only this one conundrum in sorting mail: two identical names, the teenage Madeira Mae Smith who lived just across the tracks from the post office and one house short of the Quarters, and the first grade teacher Madeira Mae Smith who lived on Rural Route One about fifteen miles away. Miss Tyndall could recognize the handwriting of any correspondents as easily as her own face in the mirror. Not a lot of first-class mail came through her post office. Faces and names were engraved in her steel-trap memory. Nothing concerning mail ever escaped the hawkeyed Miss Tyndall. She knew postmarks—even outside Brownville, Alabama.

So this current problem was not hers at all, as she saw it. She, like all other postal workers, had taken a civil service exam to establish her credentials. Miss Tyndall was pretty sure the young Madeira Mae, whom everyone called Mydearie Mae, had never been outside Tuscaloosa County in her entire life. Who could she possibly know in Detroit? If there was a mistake at all, it had to be with the sender of this letter. Miss Tyndall's only mistake, as she saw it, had been in questioning Mydearie Mae about the letter. The young are eternally optimistic: Mydearie Mae's flushed face and outburst demanding the letter said it all. Obviously, Mydearie Mae knew no one in Detroit, but she yearned for it to be so.

Today Miss Tyndall woke up early, determined and assured. For one moment yesterday she had considered asking the mail carrier, Mr. Hobson, who truly knew everyone in the county. But she knew stationery. She picked up the rumpled envelope. This was not the quality paper one would choose to write a personal note to a schoolteacher. Holding the #10 envelope up to the light had revealed none of the contents, but she squinted again just to be sure.

She was not above using steam, but there was a less criminal solution in this case. The envelope was addressed in blue ink. Miss Tyndall chose a ballpoint pen and carefully squeezed in a blue "Rural Route One" on the second line which roughly imitated the other clipped handwriting. And since she wasn't at all sure she had done the right thing about the mysterious letter, she now felt compelled to do the right thing and pin up the newest Wanted poster. Jimmy Clyde. She'd like to wad it up and trash it. Jimmy Clyde had taken better care of her car than any mechanic she'd ever had, including a weekly cleaning of the floor mats.

***

"Miss Madeira! Miss Madeira! Wake up, it's me. Jimmy Clyde."

Miss Madeira had fallen asleep early on the sofa reading the latest Grace Livingston Hill book, her reward after doling out Dick and Jane all day. She could lose herself, become the naive heroine of a historical romance who finds her wonderfully handsome, if wayward, lover and reforms him so that they live happily and easily ever after. Miss Madeira could forget briefly that the whole county considered her, at forty-two, an old maid, as did she herself.

Jimmy Clyde had the look of a raccoon wrestled out of a tree by a coon dog, wild with his red ducktail haircut hanging in his face. His jeans were covered with mud and beggar's lice. He panted to catch his breath. Sweat glistened on his face even in the half-light of the yellow porch bulb.

"Can I rest here tonight, please ma'am, and maybe get a piece of bread or a cracker?" He nearly slumped to the step but braced himself against the door. "Just till daybreak. "He slid slowly down onto the doorstep. "I'm weak. Can't run no more. Been hiding in Sipsey swamp for two days. Got no place else to go. They've got dogs and guns."

Miss Madeira was completely caught off guard. She'd never had a man of any age show up at her door in the middle of the night. She had never seen anyone who had been hiding in the swamp for two days. She had heard through the school grapevine that Jimmy Clyde had beat up and cut the mail carrier in the Brownville commissary. But she knew how a molehill-sized rumor could grow into a mountain. Also, she began to recall the hero of the romance she had just finished, of the possibilities inherent in this unexpected happenstance. She took Jimmy Clyde's arm firmly and asked him to come in, flipped off the porch light, and deadbolted the door behind them.

"I never have guests, so the room might be a little dusty." Miss Madeira turned back the white chenille spread to the foot of the bed and folded down the crisp white sheets. The lightly starched and ironed pillowcases were embroidered along the edge with a green leafy design.

Jimmy Clyde had never seen such a fine bed, much less slept in one. She handed him her daddy's old pajamas and a robe to wear while his clothes and shoes were airing on the porch. He'd stripped there before entering the bedroom. He quickly shut the door, taking care that it was loud enough for her to hear from the front room. Everything was in its place for a single guest: the oversized oval bar of soap, one white towel, and its matching washcloth embroidered with MM, just as if she had prepared the bathroom for a single guest. He saw none of the dust she'd mentioned. Emerging from the shower, he took the towel carefully, dried his face first, and then, without warning, he started sobbing. He wadded the fluffy towel and covered his face up to bury the sounds of something washing over him like the howl of a cornered animal.

Dressed now in her daddy's clothes, he smelled a faint rosy smell, and the robe felt soft snuggled up around his neck. He heard her gentle knock.

"Come in," he said and then repeated it a little louder for fear no words had come out.

"Sit down," she said, picking up a large book from the blue chaise with brocade pillows. "This room is for my projects. Make yourself at home."

She laid the art history book on the nightstand.

"This sure is nice, Ma'am," said Jimmy Clyde, fingering the gold threads on a pillow.

"Tried needlework once. Crewel and embroidery were about as far as I got." Madeira Mae pointed above the chest to a framed morning glory vine in crewel on a fence. This is one I actually finished.

She traced the morning glory design with her finger.

"But I never got around to learning to crochet or knit."

There was a catch in her voice.

"Ah, but I did try quilting once, too."

"My mama quilted," Jimmy Clyde whispered.

"Here's half of the quilt top I started. Broken Star." She laid the quilt top back in a cardboard box bulging with scraps.

"Mostly string quilts." He said it as if he were talking to himself.

Madeira glanced at the unfinished canvas sitting on an easel.

"I've tried a lot of things, but I'm not really that good at anything."

Jimmy Clyde pointed to the canvas, mostly several shades of blue with clouds and a sliver of brown at the bottom. "What about that?"

"That? Watercolor lessons. Hopeless. That thing's been sitting here for two years, and I haven't gotten beyond a sky yet. Actually, I can't get a sky I'm happy with," she mused, staring at the puffy clouds, some purplish-pink, and some tinged with gray clouds that looked too perfectly formed.

***

Miss Madeira gathered up Jimmy Clyde's clothes he had folded neatly on the front porch and put them into the washer before she went to bed. She set the table for two for breakfast and checked to be sure she had eggs. She was an early riser.

The next morning she quietly mixed up a batch of blueberry muffins and set the eggs out of the refrigerator. Then she went outside and hung Jimmy Clyde's clean clothes on the line. It was warm and bright already, a cloudless sky. The raveling threads at the bottom of his pants legs tugged at her. She looked back at the clothesline and thought how strange it seemed to have a pair of men's boxer shorts pinned up with clothes pins, to have pinned those print boxers up there herself. The first ever since her daddy died. She felt her face warming. She was glad she had no immediate neighbors and that her house was set well back off the road.

"Morning, Miss Madeira."

"Good morning, Jimmy Clyde."

She had not heard him come in and hoped her face was not flushed.

"Sun'll have your clothes dried in no time."

"But you shouldn't have done that," he protested.

22

Probably not, she thought. She felt timid and didn't know what to say.

He went on, "I was dead asleep until some mighty good smells woke me up."

He ate his three sunny side up eggs with bacon, and blueberry muffins the way her daddy used to. She sat across from him and watched him eat with the same hungry relish her Daddy did—as if it might be his last meal. The same satisfaction of draining that last sip of coffee from the second cup.

"You were wrong, Miss Madeira."

"Wrong?"

"'Bout not being good at anything. You're good at a lot of things."

Madeira Mae felt her face glowing again.

"Besides cooking, I mean. You're mighty good at teaching kids how to read. Even me. Anybody around here'll tell you you're the best first grade teacher there ever was. And not a teacher in the school could top your bulletin boards."

"Want some more coffee, Jimmy Clyde?" Miss Madeira had to separate herself from the source of heat that was building in her. She poured herself a glass of water before returning to the table with his fresh cup of coffee. How good it was to have the little kitchen table filled up again.

She sat down. The Ginger Lilies were early this year. Their sweet smell wafted through the screen door. She and Jimmy Clyde both looked out the bay window across the wide lawn above the thick bed of white blossoms and the trees in the distance.

The quiet began to feel awkward to her.

"Not a cloud in the sky this morning," she said.

"If you ever got one you were completely happy with, would you want to sell it?" asked Jimmy Clyde.

"One what?"

"A sky, like you said last night."

Miss Madeira laughed out loud.

"Sell one of my skies? Why, I couldn't give one away."

***

His promise, his promise? Miss Madeira lay the rumpled envelope on the nightstand. Was she losing her mind? What had Jimmy Clyde promised her? She looked up at the *watercolor* on the easel where a semblance of her lay stretched out on the white wicker chaise lounge with blue cushions. A lacy white scarf, truly a sheer borrowed from one of the living room windows, serpentined its way along her body, covering what needed to be covered. Or nearly. One triangular breast jutted out. Nor was the face hers either. Added last, it was a mask, a pterodactyl's head, he had said, shrunk some. But what promise had Jimmy Clyde made her? She couldn't remember any promise he'd made except that he would never, cross his heart and hope to die, tell anyone she had posed for him for this painting.

And what had she promised him? She told him she would try to find a print of "*Les Demoiselles d'Avignon*," but she didn't recall putting that in the form of an honest-to-God promise. For a whole afternoon he had carried the art history book around, staring at Picasso's five women, muttering about anatomy and muscles and angles and curves and how his whittled figures were angular and boxy, just like these women, not curvy like human flesh. He was consumed with the similarities between the five Picasso women and his whittled women. It was that night that he'd begun the watercolor of Miss Madeira.

And what could this bus ticket mean? It was one way. Was Jimmy Clyde suggesting that she give up her teaching job after all these years? What would everyone at the school think?

***

Years later it would seem to Mydearie Mae that every lesson she had ever learned in life was from the school of hard knocks. Or while exercising. She walked briskly in a near-run pace with her arms swinging wide, circling the upstairs gym. After about forty minutes of it, she had reached that euphoric state when a certain mindlessness set in. She could walk forever. Surely her legs would walk her all the way back as far as Brownville, if she ever cared to go back there again.

Funny. She rarely thought about Brownville now that her relatives were all dead or living in Northport. A woman walking with a cane had just hobbled onto the track and something about her straight back reminded Mydearie of someone—that and the way she held her chin up. When Mydearie Mae passed her the third time, she turned to get a good look at the woman's face. Sure enough, she had the mole on her forehead like Miss Tyndall, but the rest of the face didn't fit.

Now that was a name that hadn't occurred to her in a very long time. The day in the post office when Mydearie Mae confronted Miss Tyndall about the mysterious letter, and then saw the Wanted poster with her childhood sweetheart and fiancé, Jimmy Clyde, pictured, she knew Brownville was a place to walk away from. To run away from. Mortified. That's how she'd felt, mortified. Walk, run, flying would have been better that day. Too bad she couldn't fly like Jimmy Clyde.

The year she was going into third grade, her family had moved to Brownville. It was early fall after the cotton and corn fields were laid by. Her daddy had been a sharecropper all his adult life, but he left it behind to work

26

on the white pole yard. The following spring Jimmy Clyde jumped from one tree limb to another and actually caught a robin in his hands. He ran all the way from the orchard, through Shotgun Town, down the main road, and to her house with the robin cupped in his hands. The image of that bird and Jimmy Clyde's proud face had stayed with her long after he flew the coop to Detroit. So be it. Maybe she couldn't fly, but she could walk. And when she was walking, she could pretend she didn't remember. Pretend she knew nothing about that Wanted poster. Walk right out.

Walking definitely helped during her two years as a new bride. She started off studying art at the University of Alabama but her practical side kicked in. What kind of a job could you get with a degree in art? So she switched majors. Following her degree in Interior Design, she decided to apply at Rich's Department Store in Atlanta. The publicity poster had an old newspaper photograph of Margaret Mitchell standing in front of a seated Helen Norris, waiting for an autograph of Norris's book. Norris, a writing student of Hudson Strode's in the forties, was being honored with a luncheon in Atlanta. It was that poster and the idea of working in the big city that she had seen burned at least three or four times on television that intrigued Mydearie Mae. She had no idea, though, how she'd get to Atlanta or where she'd live or how she'd eat, but she knew she was good at walking. She had walked five miles each day to and from the University campus for four years over to the Kut & Kurl. There she caught a ride back to Brownville with her niece, Josie Elaine, a licensed cosmetologist.

Walk before you run. Mydearie Mae rewound the exercise tape and adjusted her headset. For two years after she got the job at Rich's, she walked up and down eight flights to a tiny cubbyhole of an apartment with four sets of locks. She walked to the bus stop and back twice a day. She walked to the elevator of Rich's that took her to the bargain basement until she was gradually promoted from sales into customer service as department head. It seemed she had a knack for soothing ruffled feathers, even those of irate Yankees visiting Dahlonega or Callaway Gardens, or going on down to Savannah or Sea Island. Her secret was just to get them to slow down. That was half the battle. Slowing down was a necessity in understanding her accent.

Aaron would never let her forget how awful he thought her southern drawl sounded. His daddy was Mydearie Mae's building superintendent in Atlanta, so she met Aaron right away. She also had a knack for sizing up men, whether they were artistic and creative, never mind their shortfalls. Aaron was less artistic and creative than any man she'd ever met. That was good. She wanted nothing to do with the likes of a Jimmy Clyde ever again. Jimmy Clyde! Rat. Deserter.

A Tale of Three Women

Shortly after meeting Aaron, she walked into the courthouse to marry him. But many times at the first of each month when Aaron demanded receipts for every cent she'd spent, even lunches, she wanted to run. He, himself, felt free to spend a fortune on his diving hobby, but she had to limit her long-distance calls to her sister, Lejeune. That cost was peanuts compared to his one wet suit. After considering her only option, going back to Northport to live with Lejeune, she always seemed to end up *crawling* back to Aaron.

Mydearie Mae adjusted her headset. *Always warm up by stretching the quadriceps and hamstrings.* The tape droned in her ear. Mydearie Mae had stretched but, honestly, stretching had not helped her marriage very much. Aaron's mother had vowed to disown him from the start, and things got worse. Trying to mix Jewish Rosenthalls and Baptist Smiths, Mydearie Mae found, was worse than mixing preachers and prostitutes at a dinner table.

A way to *walk* out finally presented itself. Mydearie Mae went downstairs to the Chanel counter to purchase a new Ruby Slipper lipstick, and one of the visiting makeup artists told her about a position she'd heard about at Parisian's in Birmingham. A design opportunity at their premiere store. She knew Aaron would never leave Atlanta, but she had had enough burglaries and drunks and street preachers and perverts to last her a lifetime. Birmingham might not be perfect, but she was hungry for someplace close to home's unlocked doors and young turnip greens cooking inside.

Avoid getting shin splints or you won't ever want to walk again. Mydearie Mae had heard a similar warning from a swimming instructor: *Get back into the deep water or you'll never get in again.* Aaron's family liked to vacation on the Gulf, and Aaron specifically liked to explore coral reefs all over the world, so Mydearie Mae had desperately wanted to overcome her fear of deep water. Her instructor made this little concession: Mydearie Mae could do her ten-minute free-style part of the swimming test in the shallow end of the Olympic-sized pool. But when it became obvious that others being tested would interrupt her, Mydearie Mae decided to try swimming the length of the pool, too. The side stroke on the first lap was fine; it was when she made that turn at the end of the pool, when she flipped over for the backstroke, that water sheeted her face and she panicked. She went straight to the bottom of the deep end and began walking toward the ladder. Her lungs were so walled by water, and her legs so shaky she could hardly pull herself up to the first rung. As she stood on the ladder gasping for breath, the instructor started in on her.

"Go on. Get back into the water. You must. If you don't, you'll never get in again. Go on. You can do it," she said, gesturing with both hands.

A Tale of Three Women

Mydearie Mae still had the certificate she earned hanging on the wall to show her competency in swimming. Its frame is black with a thin rim of brass that reflects the gold lettering of her name. This she has hanging in her bedroom. She threw out the marriage certificate along with all the other framed photos of her and Aaron on beaches that she couldn't distinguish, rocky beaches, snowy white beaches, beaches with mountains in the background—all of them she stripped from the walls and threw, one by one, into the dumpster near their building when she packed to leave Atlanta.

And she has never gone back once. Just as the swimming instructor warned, the fear of that deep water grew too great. In Birmingham she took back her maiden name. She also took up walking instead of swimming.

***

There is no hierarchy in the locker room. Mydearie Mae had waited on the post office steps every day for two weeks. Each day she had waited while Miss Tyndall got the mail sorted and pushed into all the little cubicles. Miss Tyndall could not be interrupted while she was doing that job. If you didn't have a post office box, you had to wait for your mail. While Mydearie Mae waited, she thought about Jimmy Clyde. One minute she was so mad at Jimmy Clyde she could freely kill him, and the next minute, she could hardly wait to get the letter he promised when he got up to Detroit to his brother's. She was waiting for some word from him. She knew exactly why he broke into the commissary. In fact, she was waiting outside in the car and ducked down when Mr. Hobson drove up and went inside. Mr. Hobson, she was sure, figured Clyde for a robber.

Had the whole world gone crazy? If Jimmy Clyde wanted money out of the cash register, why would he wait to break in at night when money could stick to his hands any day he worked there? And had Jimmy Clyde gone crazy? Did he think for one minute anybody in his right mind would believe that somebody broke the glass in the commissary door just to steal a whittled pterodactyl? And where was God? What would it have hurt if Mr. Hobson had not seen Jimmy Clyde? And why the mail carrier? Why not the healthy-as-a-horse night watchman at the plant? Everybody knew Mr. Hobson had a bad heart. An accidental stab in the hand with a pocketknife alone couldn't have killed anybody.

Anyway, how bad is it if somebody takes back something that is rightfully theirs in the first place, something he had whittled out with his own two hands?

Questions like this sometimes still plagued Mydearie Mae as she walked the track, especially on a dark, cloudy day like this one.

***

Another Madeira Mae was making her way carefully through the Nautilus machines at the same time. It was the first time in Miss Madeira's life she had been in a gym to work out. Every now and then someone would pass her who smelled like a child after recess on the playground, that fresh damp smell of hair not gone rank yet. She felt that she had entered another country here in this gym where people spoke a strange language and relished sweat and body odor. She had scheduled a trainer on Mondays and Wednesdays. Strength training had been recommended by her gynecologist as a deterrent to osteoporosis. She would try the low impact water aerobics class tomorrow morning.

Low, low impact, like her lifetime of teaching first graders. With that one exception— that one short happy week which she harbored in her heart for low moments, to pull out again and examine and remember detail by detail until her face warmed. Her week with Jimmy Clyde.

The path from her home on Mormon Road fifteen miles the other side of Brownville to Greystone in Birmingham had been an unexpected and crooked one. This was her last stop before Moore's Bridge Cemetery, an eerie place the last time she'd gone for the annual decoration of graves. Her tombstone was already there, with her birthdate, July 9. Most of the graves were overgrown with saw briars and Johnson grass and littered with acorns, pinecones, and sweet gum balls. The few families who lived nearby had their plots meticulously landscaped. Miss Madeira's family plot, too, had been mysteriously weeded and so freshly raked that the rake marks were still evident. Puzzling. Maybe a former student had cleaned it off. She read her epitaph out loud, the one her baby sister had suggested, "She tried."

And she definitely had. She had taught ninety per cent of the population of Brownville in the first grade. She had read enough Dick and Jane stories that she winced even now to meet someone with those names. Her lungs probably still had a good coating of chalk dust even twenty years later. Her work was her life until the night Jimmy Clyde knocked on her door.

It had been a few years since she taught Jimmy Clyde in first grade. His family lived in Shotgun Town. Her knowledge of him was limited, but singular. His flaming red hair wasn't easy to forget, nor his artistic talents. Unlike most first-grade doodling, he might render an exact duplicate of a dinosaur. He also drew birds. The cardinal and the robin he could draw from memory. Once after his mother died, he brought a gift for her to class whittled from cedar: a handsome squirrel whose tail was so lifelike, you could almost see it swinging. The intercom crackled throughout the Birmingham sports facility.

"Phone call at the front desk for Madeira Mae Smith. Madeira Mae Smith, please come to the front desk."

***

Mydearie Mae was nearly to the end of the walking track and she had listened to the exercise tape twice, so she grabbed up her towel, dried her brow, and hurried to the stairs going down. Surely her secretary at Parisian's hadn't had a problem with the fashion show scheduled for noon. She had heard there was a big push on to sell Parisian's. Yesterday every possible detail was worked out, including special seats for the big wigs coming in from Saks in Atlanta.

Simultaneously, and at the same gym, Miss Madeira's trainer looked at her and said, "Go ahead. Take the call. I'll wait." He gave her a hand off the abs machine. Her lower back was weak from years of sitting behind her first-grade school desk. She had been here at the gym less than an hour, but it was probably her baby sister, already checking on her. Probably calling to see if she'd had the big one yet.

Both Madeira Mae Smiths arrived at the front desk at the same time. After some polite confusion, the girl at the desk handed the phone to the older one. Miss Madeira's baby sister wanted her to pick up a loaf of Three Seed Bread at the Big Sky Bakery on the way home.

***

Two women dressed in workout clothes are walking down the hall together, smiling and sharing a little personal biography of the kind one gives to strangers inadvertently thrown together by some little synchronicity of life. One woman looks to be about fifteen or twenty years older than the other one. The women both giggle a little self-consciously because they have each stopped their exercise routine to respond to the same phone call at the front desk.

The two women speak briefly of the smallness of the world, of how two women with the very same name have come from the very same county and the very same postal district and end up years later at the very same gym exercising. They discuss the merits of exercise, the younger one much more convinced of its benefits.

Quite offhandedly the younger one remarks how life is so much like walking or jogging around the walking track.

"No matter how far people travel, they usually end up right back at home," the younger one says.

The older one smiles but does not respond. She knows that you can't go home again.

Unless the two bump into each other again exercising, or unless their carts collide in the produce department of the local grocery store, they may never meet again. But as they part without exchanging telephone numbers or addresses, each separately and privately generalizes about life, how people usually end up back at home, or can't. Both women wonder what ever happened to a redheaded boy named Jimmy Clyde and whether he will ever come back home to Brownville.

Part 2

Darlin', You Can't Love Two

James C. Slowe had just begun to carve out the scales on his mermaid's slender wooden body when his wife Betsy flung the back door open. She stood for a moment as if to brace herself against the warmth and light and smells of the kitchen. Her face was blotched red after walking home from the Carnegie Library in Detroit where she worked. Snow and sludge left from the weekend storm dripped from her as she peeled off her layers of clothing—hat, scarf, sweater, and coat—and hung them in the adjoining laundry room. She sat down on a low stool to take off her boots. Her short blonde hair was molded into the shape of her wool hat. She shook her hair vigorously and shouted, "Not one more marrow-freezing winter here. I'm going home."

Home for Betsy was Gordo, Alabama, a place where the infrequent light snowfall was applauded and wished for by children and most adults, just as it was in his homeplace across the county line, Brownville. Those who remembered the great snow during the depression, however, like James's parents, cringed to see a single snowflake. His daddy had measured that snowfall right at eighteen inches.

"We didn't know whether we'd freeze first, or starve to death," his daddy always said.

James had never imagined he might live in Gordo, but he looked over his shoulder, and smiled. Betsy wouldn't expect him to stop to greet her while he was working. Years of living together had acquainted them with the eccentricities of the other. He abhorred being interrupted while working. For him wood carving was a lone occupation, sometimes attracting an audience, but in his case, he wanted no interaction with onlookers.

Going home. Betsy's phrase kept coming back to him though. *Going Home.* West of Tuscaloosa and halfway between the Sipsey Swamp and Carrollton, Gordo was a southern town of no particular distinction. The only traffic through Gordo on Highway 82 was either gamblers on their way to the Mississippi riverboats or ghost-stalkers on the way to Carrollton to see its one notable sight, the famed courthouse window. Main Street had waned, and the only business ever conducted there was fast food, cheap jewelry, or wigs that looked like wigs.

For James the distinction for that area would always be the swamp; its night sounds of owls and an occasional squall of a bobcat came back to James at night. The nightmare always ended with his being sucked down into the murky undergrowth, and what his wife could only describe as a hell-raising scream.

James laid his carving knife aside and took the Fighting Rooster from his pocket. He opened the longest blade, thinned from years of sharpening. He nicked away a tiny sliver of redheart around the mermaid's cheek. The feel of this wood always pleased him as did the weight of his pocketknife. It was the first whittling knife he'd ever owned. He'd never created a piece without using it at least once, no matter how extensive or sophisticated his knife collection had become. The Fighting Rooster straightened out any kinks in his thinking. It also reminded him who he was and where he'd started.

He brushed the wood shavings from the mermaid's cherry base and got up to stir the simmering pot of beef stew. He heard Betsy washing her hands. She'd want to eat soon. As he set out two place settings, his mind was still on Gordo. More a thoroughfare than a city, Gordo was a place people moved away from, not back to. But he knew his wife better than he knew her town. Betsy had just announced that she was going back to Gordo. Once she'd said she was going back, the idea was on her list. And once it was on her list, it was as certain as her practiced crochet stitches: he might as well give away the snow shovel.

***

Betsy's trump card was perseverance, but she had had one snowstorm too many. That first wonderland season in Detroit had lost its luster after the first power outage. She had endured wearing dark-colored clothes and layering with silk thermal underwear and slogging through melting snow and salt for thirty years for only one reason, James Slowe.

His pocketknife had first thrown them together in the library when she was still working at an entry level position. Her degree in library science had not gleaned a single job offer back home, so she eagerly accepted a job at the information desk up front. James worked the day shift at the Ford assembly plant. Nights he studied at the library to get a GED. That night Betsy was struggling to open a small, but well-taped box. James walked up, set his armload of books down on the counter, whipped out his red knife, and slit the box open for her. Opening the box was as easy as snipping a piece of sewing thread with an Exacto knife.

It was his fascination with the knife that Betsy first found riveting. He opened and closed each of its four blades one by one before putting it back into his pocket. Light in this old library was not too good unless you were reading by one of the floor lamps or directly under a table lamp, but even so, the knife blades deflected the light and made it dance as if they had been polished and recently sharpened on a whetstone to a silver thinness. Betsy had a healthy fear of sharp blades ever since she sliced her left forefinger open with her daddy's knife trying to sharpen a pencil. The size of this knife unnerved her, but she gritted her teeth and thanked James for his help. Quite honestly, she had grown weary of always playing it safe.

Betsy had no best friend here yet and felt mostly ignored by everybody. Men and women in this city avoided any direct eye contact. Only if they needed library help, and that was fine with her. Sometimes she wondered why she had totally lost track of her college buddies who were mostly from the rural south. It was common knowledge that once a girl is out of college, without a Mr. Right, she is on her way to becoming a lifelong old maid. The men she'd met here were hopeless in one way or another, not a single prospect for dinner, much less taking home to meet her parents.

Before meeting James, she had decided that given a certain period of time, she might just move back to Gordo, even without a job. She sometimes longed to work in the children's department in Detroit where the mothers came in for story hour, their toddlers bundled up like little fat pink or blue rabbits, or their infants hanging in safe cozy slings next to the chests of their mothers. She could almost feel the nearness of an extra little heartbeat, the round head cuddled to her breast.

How frigid would a lifetime be here, unmarried and childless? Still, as hard as she tried, she was never able to convince herself to go back. Somehow living with her parents in the old Gordo farmhouse set in the middle of a cotton field didn't seem very enticing and certainly not promising—playing the piano at the Methodist church on Sunday mornings and Wednesday nights; picking and canning vegetables in the summer with no air conditioning; winter nights crocheting or knitting while her mother pieced quilt scraps and her daddy whittled tops out of empty thread spools by the fireplace. Thus the litany: days and seasons and years ticking by, as monotonous as the old clock sitting on the mantel. In the light of that bleak future, what would a little risk with this knife-loving stranger hurt?

She had agreed to meet James in the food court of the building across the street after work. She ordered Moo Goo Gai Pan, and he got a large pepperoni pizza. They ate and chattered, mostly the minutiae exchanged by strangers. Turned out, he was from Brownville, not twenty miles away from Gordo. They both laughed out loud at the odds of that coincidence. They knew very few people in common, for only a few family names had drifted across county lines, the Pooles, the Frees, and the Mullinaxes, and she'd had one old maid distant cousin she'd never met, a Smith she thought, who had taught first grade at the same school near Brownville all her life. Did James know her, Betsy wondered.

James put the half-eaten slice of pizza down.

"Her name started with *M*, I think. Madeira Mae. That's it. Madeira Mae Smith."

James suddenly started coughing and excused himself from the table. He had swallowed a whole piece of pepperoni and came as close to choking to death on a piece of food as he ever had. He continued to cough loudly in the bathroom until his throat was cleared. By then his forehead was beaded with sweat. A distant cousin. Old maid schoolteacher. Named Smith. Who else but Miss Madeira? His head reeled with the shock of remembering, and waves of nausea were rocking his stomach. Flashbacks of darkness, and cold swamp water, and dogs barking and the loud squalls of a

45

bobcat as he slumped exhausted and half-crazed in the crook of a cypress tree. James leaned over the sink and splashed cold water up on his face. He looked in the mirror and swiped his brow with a paper towel. His dark brown hair continued to surprise him. He leaned into the mirror and saw the bright red roots. Oh, hell, he was going to have to use more dye.

James told Betsy the pizza was not setting well on his stomach, that he had an ulcer and sometimes he had severe reactions to food. Which was not exactly a lie. Onions could put him on his knees in pain. He left the food court immediately. What if Betsy had already heard about him or maybe even recognized him? What if he had to run somewhere else and start over again?

God, how he still ached to see his sweetheart, Mydearie Mae. Why the hell hadn't she used that bus ticket he sent her? Why hadn't she at least written him back? It didn't add up. He'd kept his promise and sent her the one-way ticket. Her promise was to follow him to Detroit and not a single word. Hell, she probably decided she was too good to run off with him. Or she got the big head about college and forgot all about this old Brownville boy. He looked around, then kicked a tire of a car parked on the street so hard it bruised his big toe through his safety boots.

The next morning on the assembly line, he went over the details of that last night he and Mydearie Mae had in Brownville together. He saw her smiling face, not the tires he affixed to the moving car frame on the assembly line—her nearly-black wavy hair, and eyes as green as a new apple. Thinking back on that two weeks before he managed to thumb his way north was like getting on a nightmarish see-saw swinging up to a devilish height, being scared and furious enough to shit nails, then flopping to the ground so homesick he'd double over, crying. Homesick is one thing, but when you know you can't ever go home again, now that will nearly claw the bottom of your gut open.

He began to escape those thoughts by shifting his mind in another direction as he worked—he'd imagine building a person with car parts as the frame moved along; sometimes his two tires would be legs, and the two on the other side would be arms; sometimes he'd imagine a whole body built from tires. He knew it was certifiable, but he'd imagine what parts of this tire person he could whittle from wood, maybe a maple head, or cedar arms. Even his imaginary whittling, however, could not totally erase his past.

A lot of young people from around Brownville fled the south hoping for a better life. Some went to Illinois, some, to Michigan. Rumor had it there was always work on the assembly lines. It was actually Miss Madeira, the teacher who apparently was Betsy's cousin, who first suggested Detroit. Thinking back on it, that whole week with her when he was on the run was a dream, the kind of dream you don't want to wake up from, but you know that if you don't, an alarm is going to go off too late. Until his dying day James would never forget how clean her guest bed was, how white its sheets were, how they smelled of sweet sun and Ginger Lilies, the embroidered and ironed pillowcases, the watercolor he painted....

"You moved your arm. Crook the elbow back, closer to your head. Gotta make this look like ax strokes."

"You're actually smiling, Jimmy Clyde. See there. You can be happy again. Quit blaming yourself for the accident."

"That's a heck of a lot easier said than done," he said, *leaning in close to the canvas, and then looking back at Picasso's five women.*

"We should go easier on ourselves for mistakes."

"Think Picasso ever made any mistakes?" he asked.

"*Everybody does. But God can forgive, and if God can, surely we can forgive ourselves.*" *She shifted herself a little on the chaise.*

"*Aw, Miss Madeira, you're just saying that to make me feel better.*"

No, not at all. Look it up. It's in Deuteronomy. There were cities of refuge for men who might accidentally kill another man, let's say with an ax while chopping a tree down."

"*I'd like to be hiding out in this Avignon, wherever it is.*" *He swirled the blob of paint on the palette with his brush.*

"*Detroit's a lot closer,*" *she said.*

"*Let me move the lace over your chest, Miss Madeira. There, that's it, that's it. . .*"

To imagine that this Betsy librarian was kin to his former first grade teacher and friend, Miss Madeira, made his face go as red as his hair roots. Painting Miss Madeira nude was not what he hated at all—he could picture himself eating her good breakfast, with the smell of the coffee and the Ginger Lilies all mixed up. It was *why* he ended up hiding out at her house that he hated. Mr. Hobson's death. Mr. Hobson was such a good person, too. Did Betsy know about his death? James was not a person to let a thing go unresolved.

And he knew just how to do it. The next night
James walked briskly into the library holding a large
bulky armful of something wrapped in what
appeared to be a white sheet. He walked straight up
to her counter, set it down, and started to unwind
the white cloth. Betsy was aware that a few of the
regular patrons were glancing up, those who came
in from the cold to snooze in a comfortable chair or
to flip through the magazines.

A warm, reddish pterodactyl emerged with
wings partially extended. Its talons were perched on
a wooden base, but it appeared to be in half-flight.
The wood was polished to a soft shine.

"My prize piece," he said, smiling.

He watched Betsy's eyes carefully for any sign
of recognition that she had heard about it before. If
she knew about Mr. Hobson, she would know his
pterodactyl. She simply looked stunned.

"Honduras mahogany," he explained further.

Betsy took her time gazing at every detail of the
piece and finally said, "Amazing." She ran a finger
along a ribbed wing.

It was as if she could only muster up that one
word.

"Base is cherry," he said to fill the empty air. "It's
my mark."

Betsy drew in a deep breath. "Where in the world did you learn how to do this?"

"I didn't. My Fighting Rooster does it for me. I just hold the handle. This old boy makes whittling a bird or squirrel as easy as sliding down a greased pole," he said, pulling the knife from his pocket.

"Pardon the pun," said Betsy, "but I think this is a cut above whittling."

A man had risen from his armchair and shuffled up to the counter. He had long wavy hair and a nervous tic that made his whole head shake periodically.

"Man, what kinda mothafucker monster bird is that?" the man said, reaching out toward the carving which was now completely unveiled from the sheet.

"Hey, hey now, hands off...," said James, sliding the pterodactyl safely out of his reach. "And you shut your foul mouth, you hear me?"

"Whatchu mean...?"

Before the man could utter another sound, James flipped the longest blade open and snatched a handful of the man's hair, jerking his head backwards. The tip of the blade he held taut to the man's exposed throat.

"You wanna watch the last drop of your blood gush out of your nasty-talking throat, man?" James growled in a low tone. "Or do I have to stick you like a pig so's you can sweeten your tongue the next time you're in the company of a lady? Your choice, mister."

The man turned mute. Betsy held her breath praying his nervous tic would still itself.

"Smart man," hissed James. "Remember this lesson," he said, barely nicking the man's skin with the knife.

Betsy gasped as she pressed the buzzer for security. She saw a small trickle of blood ooze out. She pressed the buzzer again and again. Hans came lumbering down the aisle from the reference room.

"Got a little nasty problem here, eh, Miss Betsy?" asked Hans, grabbing each man by the arm. "Youse sorry slobs, git on outta here. Out. Git on out." Hans was tall and probably weighed as much as the two of them together. He chuckled as he manhandled them to the front door.

James stood and watched while the man with the nervous tic, muttering under his breath, shuffled off down the sidewalk. Then he quickly went to a side entrance and was back at Betsy's checkout counter within minutes. Betsy had already begun rewrapping the sculpture. She was more than a little spooked, but a thread of excitement inched up her backbone when she saw James coming back.

Hans was bent over admiring the details of one of the talons of the pterodactyl. He looked up at James and rolled his eyes. "Better keep outta sight, man."

James ignored Hans and turned to Betsy, who ignored them both and kept wrapping the pterodactyl. James wanted to apologize for being so crude.

"Somebody talented like you, man, don't need to be walking around, intimidating people with his instrument," said Hans, reprovingly. He winked at James but spoke loud enough for the other library visitors to hear the reprimand.

"Somethin' my daddy taught me early was that gutter talk's okay, but ladies don't need to hear it," said James. "A lot of Daddy I just can't get outta me."

"Hans and I are used to the homeless," said Betsy. "They're harmless, I think." She tried to control the nervous quiver of her lip. "Hearing whatever they say is a hazard of working with the public, I'm afraid."

Hans nodded in assent. He said quietly to James, "Say, the Woodchucks meet over in

Frankenmuth every month. Just say the word. I can get you in."

This protective outburst from James had stunned Betsy. She was not used to men with hot tempers. The men in her family would have to have their noses ground right into a brick wall to react so aggressively to defend anyone, much less a woman they barely knew. She guessed she should probably be afraid and wary of this man. Instead, his behavior was scintillating. No one had ever stood up for her like that before.

Betsy and James began to talk over pancakes or doughnuts, over hot dogs or hamburgers. James was one of those hungry types who could eat anything and still stay skinny. He was always hungry. And Betsy was hungry for James. Nobody she'd met in Detroit whittled or carved wood. Of course, James's talent was obviously way beyond what she had seen her daddy do. He had whittled just to pass the time; in much the same way she crocheted the same baby blanket pattern over and over. Row after row of chain stitch, double crochet stitch, chain stitch, double crochet stitch.... All rote, but like whittling tops from a wooden thread spool, it busied the hands on lonely nights.

James explained how his daddy was a carpenter on the side and offered him the wood scraps to practice on. James learned early that the softer woods were easier to work with, that you could make little mistakes, but correct them. The harder woods were a different matter.

"What about the pterodactyl? He's mahogany you said?"

"Honduras Mahogany. Very forgiving wood. Like you I'll bet."

Betsy felt her face redden. Was he asking forgiveness for the outburst with the knife? For someone just shy of a high school education, his logic surprised her. His reason for whittling he said was, "Can't nobody take that away from me."

"Ever thought about art school, James?"

"No money for classes."

"What about scholarships?"

"Not smart enough. I ain't even got the GED yet."

"You know you can do that."

"All I know for sure is whittling."

"Sometimes one thing's enough to know."

***

One thing was also enough for James to dream. When he was eight, he spotted a beautiful robin from his special perch in the old peach tree at the community orchard. It was a Saturday in spring and all the fruit trees were in bloom. He had been watching a bumblebee and missed seeing the robin when it first lit in the peach tree next to him. Ever since he could remember, he had dreamed of catching a robin and holding it in his hand. He wanted to examine the wings up close and learn by heart the way the feathers all fit together, and the exact shade of its red breast.

Mama was the only person he ever dared tell this dream. And his new third grade classmate, Mydearie Mae, of course. Big, big mistake telling her. She laughed him right off the playground.

"You're crazy. You can't catch a robin. You've got to fly to catch a robin." She had already told everybody in third grade how he spent more time up in a tree than he did on the ground. "Like some old big-lipped monkey," she told them, lolling her tongue out at him.

This was the day he'd show Mydearie Mae. The robin had not seen him yet. James eased himself up to a squatting position, leaned out, and jumped as hard as he could toward the limb on the tree where the robin perched, keeping both eyes on the bird. He hit the ground so hard it felt like his tail bone had cracked his ribs, but when he looked down to his cupped hands, the robin was looking back at him.

He ran with his tail bone aching all the way through Shotgun Town, ran down the main street and past the commissary, running to Mydearie Mae's house. She was outside pumping water.

It was a moment made as permanent as the carved and initialed heart for Mydearie Mae on the peach tree. Anytime he was scared, or aching, or bored with the assembly line, or homesick for Brownville, he tried to recall that moment of holding his cupped hands out to Mydearie Mae, of seeing the awe in her eyes, of believing him now to be capable of miracles. "Jimmy Clyde, you did it. You can fly," she had said. Then he held his hands high in the air, and watched the robin soar away. Some days that moment, that look in her eyes, would play over and over in his mind like the line of a favorite song.

He had seen a similar look in Betsy's eyes now, but clearly it was only the pterodactyl that she admired, the art and not the artist. Meeting Betsy, though, definitely began to broaden both their lives. Betsy began to scour her sources for scholarships for James. On the nights she worked, she and James managed to meet at the diner near the library and talk. She told him how her family had lived in the same house on the same road in the middle of a cotton field all her life. He told her how he'd been born in Shotgun Town in Brownville and his daddy had worked on the wood yard and how he, himself, had quit school early. The part about his mama was harder, but he told Betsy how his mother had dropped dead with a stroke when he was in tenth grade. He stopped short of the history of his departure from Brownville after Mr. Hobson's unfortunate death.

One night in the library Betsy overheard James telling Hans that his daddy had fought in World War II at the Remagen Bridge and about the Purple Heart he'd earned. This information was vital. The children of veterans had access to higher education monies and Betsy could obtain the application forms for him. She had also given James an informal aptitude test. His scores pointed to both art and engineering. James didn't know that much about either profession, but he wanted the one that would get him a good-paying job the quickest.

***

The moon was not winking at all. That's the first thing Mydearie Mae noticed about the old neon sign at the Moon Winx Lodge as she drove through

Alberta City on her way to her sister's house just across the river bridge from Tuscaloosa in Northport. After thirty years the moon was still smiling, detailed with eyes, nose, mouth, and chin, cradled in the red L shaped sign: Lodge and Restaurant. It was Friday night and she was stopping for dinner there for a reunion with an old college friend. She had coupled this meeting with a few days off work to cook pear preserves with her sister, Lejeune. Preserving pears was an annual event that had started out in nostalgia for the old days when she first moved back to Birmingham from Atlanta.

The second thing Mydearie Mae noticed about the Moon Winx was how shabby and unkempt the grounds looked, the beds unweeded, and the shrubs, which used to be so neatly manicured, wild and overgrown with honeysuckle vines. Mydearie Mae mulled over the coincidence and possible significance of this random choice of the Moon Winx. Betsy had suggested it immediately as a meeting place. Convenient to both she'd said.

Betsy had been a senior in Hayden Harris, the co-op dorm, when Mydearie Mae was a freshman. Betsy remembered that the two of them teamed up for breakfast duty. Words were not needed as they set the tables, scrambled the eggs, and made the toast—as silent as Betsy's crochet hook: single crochet stitch, double crochet stitch—until time to ring the first bell.

As Mydearie Mae pulled the car into a parking space, she strained to recall other tidbits about Betsy. College seemed a lifetime away, yet their third-floor cramped room as well as the shared breakfast duty was coming back. They got along so well Mydearie Mae wondered why they had not stayed in touch. Betsy was the only girl she'd ever met who could put her hair up in rollers without a mirror. The rigid plastic kind. Hard to believe now that they had actually slept some nights in those rollers. Betsy wore very little makeup, but she had a lipstick, Dusty Rose, which Mydearie Mae coveted. Both of them were morning people, up and ready to get the daily duty over and done with. She remembered Betsy as very kind to freshmen. Helpful. Fascinated with the sociology major next door and her "book." Shrieking at the illustrations of possible sex positions. Talking of marriage and babies. Flipping pages furiously. Innocence lost.

Mydearie Mae had reached the entrance to the Moon Winx Lodge restaurant. Reality returning. Pumpkins had been clumped about in an attempt to be festive. It was that time of the year. The night clerk inside pointed her down the hall to Cafe Luna.

A Tale of Three Women

She walked into the nearly empty cafe, and it was a little like stepping back into the coffee house on University Avenue in the sixties. Colorful Japanese paper lanterns covered the lights hanging from the ceiling over each table. Incense was burning somewhere although she hadn't seen it yet. A stack of newspapers and magazines filled a rack just inside the door. A smaller shelf held books with titles on health foods, homeopathy, food supplements, and yoga. Mydearie Mae picked up a dusty little blue book, *Searching for Ambergris*. She wondered for a second what that word meant, but then put it back down and started sniffing the sticks of incense.

No two tables were alike, all shapes and sizes and materials, as if someone had combed through garbage piles on the streets gathering tables and chairs discarded by graduating students. Yet in spite of its hodge-podge decor, there was something pleasing about the cafe and its mixture of scents. In front of the counter, which separated the kitchen from the dining area, was a shelf of at least one hundred silver tins of tea. The names were enticing—Jasmine with Flowers, Darjeeling Rington, Ceylon Lover's Leap, Imperial Gold Formosa Oolong, Flowery Orange Pekoe, and

Dragon's Heart, a house blend of Chinese Rose Black Tea and Indian Spices.

Mydearie Mae was early, so she chose a table near the tea counter and after looking at all the teas until she became bewildered, chose a simple familiar flavor, Cranberry Spice. She faced the entrance, considering what the modern-day Betsy might look like. Would they recognize each other? She quickly dismissed that niggling worry. Two women would know each other, especially college roommates.

Betsy had phoned Mydearie Mae, telling her how she pulled out the old dorm directory when she recently moved back home to Gordo, hoping to contact some of the town girls who might still live in the area. Oddly, the number of Mydearie Mae's sister, Lejeune, was penciled in the book. And by an even greater coincidence, Lejeune's phone number had never changed.

Madeira Mae saw nothing as simple coincidence. She felt that all women should trust their intuition more. And her intuition told her it was rather titillating to be here at the Café Luna, about to have some insight as to why she was here, and why Betsy was back in Gordo, and why their lives might be intersecting again, here at the Moon

Winx where she'd last eaten with Aaron Rosenthall.
Aaron Big Loser Rosenthall.

During the divorce she had tried to recall just
why she'd ever married Aaron in the first place.
Living in his hometown had appealed to her. She
had majored in Interior Design, and Atlanta was the
New York of the South. Lejeune had been dubious
from the start. She should have listened to Lejeune's
warnings. At least there had been no children. No
custody fights. Dinner that night was telling, a sign
of some kind: Aaron was totally disgusted with
every crack and crevice of the Moon Winx, with
every sprinkle of salt and sprig of parsley in the
dinner. She remembered how he'd reached across
the table and squeezed her hand, not in tenderness,
but to hurt her. His salad was overdressed and
triggered his rant. Too much parmesan in the
dressing. Why had she chosen this place? She could
never do anything right.

Betsy's marriage had apparently been just the
opposite. She had told Mydearie Mae on the phone
she had worked hard to stay married to the same
man all these years. What else could one do stuck in
a frozen tundra? Betsy explained this cheerfully.
James was an engineer, she said, but not a typical
engineer. He was very artistic, too, and designed
toys for one of the large toy companies. They

laughed about the engineers they'd double-dated once. Typically, the boys had a plastic sheath in their shirt pockets filled with mechanical pencils and a slide rule on their belts and absolutely nothing of interest to talk about.

Now, being here so many years later, Mydearie Mae couldn't help wondering what this engineer of Betsy's might look like. She glanced around the room, trying not to obviously stare. So far, no men with slide rules on their belts.

Just then a man entered the cafe alone. Needed a table for three for dinner. There was something familiar about this voice, but Mydearie Mae mustn't stare. She looked away, then back again. This was silly. What man would she know here in Alberta City? She listened without looking as he discussed drinks with the waitress. It was a southern voice but with a few words clipped. He was looking straight at her now, but she tried to look distracted.

It was Jimmy Clyde sure enough. Lord have mercy! She winced. His red hair was solid gray.

She felt faint. Just then the waitress set the teapot with the steeping tea leaves in it on her table and obstructed her view for a moment. The tea leaves are settling. *Settle yourself. Settle. Settle.* She tried to imagine herself in the yoga prayer pose.

A Tale of Three Women

A woman with a short blonde bob, crisply trimmed, approached Jimmy Clyde's table, and he half stood and pulled out the chair. She wore a green matching sweater set and a plaid kilt similar to the ones they wore in college. Oh, mercy, it was Betsy sure as the world, still attractive, a little plumper than she used to be. Still not much makeup. Wedge heels.

Jimmy Clyde and Betsy! What kind of God would let such an irony happen?

Mydearie Mae lowered her eyes. She'd wait for Betsy to make a move. She struggled for breath. Would her heart stop? Thank goodness she'd never told Betsy or anybody else in college about Jimmy. Her heart was going to burst open. What a nightmare. Maybe she was wrong. She hoped she was wrong. She was about to be sick. She peeked around the menu. So far Jimmy Clyde showed no signs of recognizing her.

"M.M.," Betsy called out, running over to her table with arms outstretched. "You're a sight for sore eyes. You've not aged one smidgen bit. Look how thin you are. And that big hair. I hate you, girl."

"Hello, M.E.," Mydearie Mae said, succumbing to the bear hug. The forgotten initials rolled off Mydearie Mae's tongue as if the two of them had lunched together or had coffee yesterday. Betsy, full name, Mary Elizabeth, had dubbed the three freshmen on third floor by their initials. It was her icebreaker. "I'm me—" she'd say, extending her bold handshake. "M.E."

She pulled Mydearie Mae to her table. "M.M. Rosenthall, meet my one and only, James C. Slowe."

Oh, this was too much of a coincidence. Betsy had obviously used the initials M.M. whenever she mentioned her name. And of course Betsy wouldn't know that she'd dropped Rosenthall for her maiden name, Smith. Mydearie Mae offered her hand. Jimmy Clyde's touch was surprisingly electric—not the soft, careful squeeze of an older man, and not the bone-crusher of the young. Now Mydearie Mae could see the panic in his face and knew that he'd had no early warning. She saw a plea in his eyes that she had seen a thousand times begging her to keep a little confidence between them. It was as appealing to her now as it had been all those years ago. A secret look. Something only they shared. The beauty of the pterodactyl he whittled. The robin he caught. The commissary accident. Her heart rate was as high as it got after twenty minutes of hard walking on the track.

She hoped Betsy wouldn't notice. She took a deep breath. Fool. Why should she let him squirm his way out of this situation? Jimmy Clyde owed her some answers. Why had he not figured out a way to get in touch with her? Why no letter? No bus ticket? Why had he simply disappeared?

***

"You just wonder whatever happened to Jimmy Clyde?" asked Lejeune. She closed up the album and put it away. "How does somebody just drop off the earth like he did?"

Lejeune was ripping open a five-pound bag of sugar. Mydearie Mae spread the mistaken murder article out on the counter. She wondered how she'd tell Lejeune about seeing Jimmy Clyde at the Moon Winx.

"Jimmy Clyde was cleared completely, you know," Lejeune continued.

Mydearie Mae looked up at her sister who was pouring sugar over the pan of peeled and sliced pears. She restrained herself although she wanted to throw her hands up and shout deliriously.

"Remember Miss Tyndall-tyrant? Her tiny kingdom of a post office is gone now." She pointed to a shot of the postmistress raising the flag. "And the article clearly proves that Mr. Hobson actually died from a heart attack."

"Jimmy Clyde is back," Mydearie Mae said, as calmly as she could manage.

"Back here?"

"Gordo, actually.

"Still available?" Lejeune teased.

"Don't imagine so. He has a new name. A wife. She's an old friend, actually."

"An old friend?" said Lejeune. "Do tell."

"Betsy. My college buddy. The one who called here to locate me. The one I met for dinner last night. They've moved back to her home in Gordo."

Mydearie Mae was speaking in an even tone, trying to control the tiny spurt of joy she felt against all odds.

"You mean he was right there at the table last night, too? What in the world did he have to say for himself?" asked Lejeune.

"What could he say? Betsy has no clue, you know."

The mound of pear peelings grew in the sink as the two sisters talked and speculated. Mydearie Mae always knew Jimmy Clyde was not a murderer. She had to admit it was good to see him again. But

A Tale of Three Women

Jimmy Clyde was married now. He was now James Slowe. She had to remember that. And he had a whole lot of explaining to do, just as Lejeune insisted. Mydearie Mae hated to think how Betsy would react if and when she was confronted with the news that her James C. Slowe used to be Madeira Mae's own Jimmy Clyde.

***

The next morning after the dinner at the Moon Winx, James was up before dawn on the back porch. He looked east toward Brownville where the sky was beginning to lighten over the stubble of a corn field.

"Jimmy Clyde, ain't no use you laying in bed all day every day. It ain't gonna bring your mama back."

"I know that, Daddy."

"Better uncover that red head when I talk to you, peckerwood. I can't make you go to school, but I can kick you outta that bed and outta my house. You better ask old man Hodo about a job."

"Don't want no job of his."

"You think you gonna make a living sleeping or whittling? What you gonna live on? Huckleberries and love?"

"Better'n peeling poles like you."

"More to life than whittling, Jimmy Clyde. Reckon there's more'n peeling poles, too. Heard tell them Poole boys got work in Detroit."

James sipped his coffee and brought himself out of the reverie. He went into his shop, which was just at the end of the back porch, set his coffee mug down, and picked up an abandoned bird's nest he found near the house. He had been asked to do a one-man art show that would be coming up in early spring at a new gallery in Northport. In addition to the mermaid, he was working on a sculpture that he was tentatively calling a self-portrait. He didn't know how he would use the bird's nest yet, but he might use it somewhere in the piece. If he was confused before about whom he was portraying in this piece, now the confusion had tripled after the jolt of seeing Mydearie Mae.

James C. or Jimmy Clyde?

James C., the engineer and artist? What one sculpture could depict such a span—from high school dropout to designer of children's toys? Some parts of the experience he had tried to symbolize with the brain, a cube made from a revolving cue ball with pockets carved out of it. One of the brain pockets had a pin-point hole at its end, which if revolved just to the precise position would line up with the left eye and let light shine through.

Jimmy Clyde, accused criminal? His right hand clutched a fluffy sky-blue scrap of lace, a reminder of the surreal week when he was harbored by his first-grade teacher, Miss Madeira, the other Madeira Mae Smith.

James C., heart patient? He'd had to have a stent put in an artery first, and then a pacemaker. To show this, he had concocted a breast made of an old tin mailbox opened to show its seam down the middle, and with a big shiny bolt holding in the wonders of the medical world.

Jimmy Clyde, who could fly?

James C. extended the Icarus-like wings to the exact width of the wings on his mahogany pterodactyl which occupied a prominent place on the bedroom lowboy. Any sculpture depicting him should have something of his most valued piece in it. He picked up some turkey feathers standing in a pencil cup and wired them to the sculpture on the one kicked-up foot, as if he were about to take flight.

Jimmy Clyde, the flaming redhead, who had a temper to match his hair, and a love for Mydearie Mae hotter than either.

James was suddenly stumped. He walked to the largest window in his shop and looked out at the rising sun. That heat was instantly rekindled last night, like a piece of coal gone gray for a few years, but suddenly red hot again as if somebody had blown hard on it, scattering its cooled ash.

James recalled the day he ran to Mydearie Mae with the robin. He got up and walked around and around in his small, familiar shop, now and then touching a carving knife or a lathe but never seeing any of it. He would not, could not, work on the sculpture today. Somehow he'd figure out how to see Mydearie Mae again after Betsy left for work.

He sat down, too saturated with voices and memories for self-examination. He picked up the elongated bird's nest, built in a pot of pansies by a Carolina Wren. The nest looked like his haystack of hair first thing in the morning. Bingo. He'd found hair for his self-portrait.

***

"Betsy's not like you, Mydearie Mae," said James, breaking the silence and daring to smooth a short wavy curl behind Mydearie Mae's ear.

It had not been terribly difficult to convince Mydearie Mae to meet him at the Moon Winx Lodge. A room at the lodge was another matter. He had requested a room on the back side away from traffic and the restaurant. But he had to admit it was extremely awkward for them both. They now sat in the motel room at a round table across from each other, trying to express in words that awkwardness. She sipped on a pot of Jasmine tea from room service, and he was drinking a Coca-Cola from the machine down the hall. The contents of his jeans pockets lay between them, including the Fighting Rooster. They had made love the way of a returning soldier, tentative at first. Now the linens of the king-sized bed looked as though a battalion had been wallowing in it. They sat quietly afterwards, each relishing the close proximity of the other.

The very first thing over the drinks was a fast and steady volley of questions and answers. He did write to her. He promised he had. His letter must have been lost. Yes, Mydearie Mae agreed. She was certain it had been the letter she argued with Miss Tyndall about right after he left. The one addressed to the first-grade teacher with the same name on Rural Route One. He had sent the one-way bus ticket. Mydearie Mae had never received it. The call she had never made because she thought he had broken his promise and did not want her in Detroit. The call he had never made out of fear of the police tracing the call. The years of pain and having to move on to survive. College for both. A job at Rich's for her and a divorce; engineering for him, and Betsy, now his good wife who had made a college degree happen.

"But Betsy's very different from you, Mydearie Mae. Marry me now, will you?"

"Everybody's different, you know. And besides, Jimmy Clyde, you're already married."

"Yes, I'm married, and I owe Betsy a lot. Frankly, I owe her my life," he said turning toward the mirror. "But you thought I could fly, remember? I think you still do."

"She doesn't?"

"She wants to, but it isn't the same. She's disappointed that there've been no children. She tries to hide it. But I see it. Who couldn't see it? She crochets baby blankets one after the other and gives them away. She doesn't even know any new mothers in Gordo, so she's nearly filled up a cedar chest. Days she escapes through her job at the hospital library. But there are always the nights. Somehow our sex is great, but it's no good."

Mydearie Mae raised an eyebrow.

"No intimacy. Just accommodation," he explained.

"Yet you aren't angry?"

"Nope. Anger's a waste. My temper's faded faster than my hair color. I'm into peace these days." He grinned and held up his fingers to make the peace sign of the sixties.

What Mydearie Mae said then was surprising, even to her. "Well, you know what? That sign is meaningless after all these years. I see little peace anywhere. I've been angry enough for both of us. I've been angry enough to slap your face. Angry enough to slap any man's face that walks by. Angry that one simple letter could ruin so many lives. Angry at life itself that in one way or another, it gives you a plateful of heartache and sorrow. No matter who you are or where you go." She was sobbing.

He was bare chested and Mydearie Mae thought how good he still looked, even though his rub board belly was a little fleshed out.

She continued, "Why didn't you try again? Try more letters? Find my address at the University? Make a phone call? How is that I only happen to meet men who are consumed more with their passions and their art than they are with the women who love them?" She dried up her eyes.

He must work out with weights. She wore his chambray shirt. Only that. She peeked out through the bright crack between the heavy curtains.

"I can't do this to any woman," said Mydearie Mae. Her voice was firm, but a pang of regret was already rising in her. For Jimmy Clyde. For the babies he would never have.

"What? What about this?" He gestured toward the rumpled bed.

Mydearie Mae sat in a straight chair. Silent. She could only think of Betsy and those crocheted baby blankets.

"Then if you won't *marry* me, can we at least meet again?"

"Jimmy Clyde, what are you suggesting? Do you know how totally miserable I would be with a cat-and-mouse kind of carrying-on?"

"If I get a divorce, I could be knocking at your door every morning in the bright daylight, no carrying-on to it."

He took both her hands in his and kissed them, then moved to her throat, planting stray kisses here and there as he began slowly to unbutton her top button. Any resolve Mydearie Mae had managed to muster up was flung farther away from her than his chambray shirt.

***

"Hello," said Mydearie Mae, answering the phone, trying hard not to sound as though she had been asleep. It was only nine-thirty at night, but she had dozed off while reading. The bedroom lights made her squint.

"Hello?" She cleared her throat and tried again.

"Mydearie Mae, it's me." It was Jimmy Clyde.

"Why are you whispering?"

"Betsy's in the shower."

"Where are you?'

"My shop."

"What's wrong?"

"Everything."

"Jimmy Clyde, I'm half asleep. Try to make sense, please."

"There's no sense. Betsy's dug in her heels. She won't give me a divorce. Here she is, back home, fifty-one, 'too dependent on you to live alone.' Betsy's exact words. Tell me, Mydearie Mae, where's the sense in that?"

"Just calm down now. Remember what you said about peace. She loves you, Jimmy Clyde. No, excuse me. She loves James C. Slowe."

"Why are you talking this way?"

"She created you. You're her pterodactyl."

"Damn it, Mydearie Mae. Whose side are you on anyway? Uh, oh. Water's stopped. Gotta go."

***

The Moon Winx had a stark look in the light of day without the romance of its neon light. Suddenly Mydearie Mae felt as tawdry as the run-down lodge. Mydearie Mae knew without knowing that Betsy knew everything now. She could hear it in Betsy's voice when Betsy phoned to ask when she would be in town again for lunch. Now she sensed a coolness about the quick hug when Betsy rose from the table-for-two to greet her. Mydearie Mae took a deep breath, pulled out the chair, and sat down. It had been easy enough when she was alone with Jimmy Clyde, but this was different. She didn't like confrontations, but what possible excuse did she have not to have lunch with Betsy?

"So-o," Betsy dragged out the word, "Mydearie Mae and my James have a past named Jimmy Clyde, do they?"

There it was. The cold truth. Betsy had laid it right out on the little round table in one short sentence without preamble. No whining, no accusing—before they could even order tea. Not angry. Not threatening. Inquisitive. As if she had been commenting on something as simple as eggs scrambled too hard or burnt toast.

"Dragon's Heart," Betsy continued, looking up to the waitress. "You, too, Mydearie Mae?"

No friendly initials today either. Mydearie Mae nodded. She'd better not rock this precarious canoe over a tea choice.

"Two Dragon Hearts," commanded Betsy.

After the waitress left, Betsy said, "I want to hear it from you."

"About our past?" Mydearie Mae asked timidly. She truly didn't like to see Betsy so upset.

"About the accident. Am I married to a murderer?"

"Thirty years, and you still can't figure that out?" quipped Mydearie Mae.

It was a question she hadn't expected and a defensive tone she hadn't intended. The details of that night in the commissary flooded over her in a flash, the dark, the fear. Jimmy Clyde couldn't bear to sell his pterodactyl at any price. He was simply going to get it back from its shelf in the commissary. Something simple grown sinister and complex. Jimmy Clyde's memory of what happened that night while she was waiting for him in the car had played over and over in her mind for years. His prying open the lock of the commissary door with the Fighting Rooster. The creaking floor of the commissary. The longest blade of his knife still open. Shining the flashlight on the pterodactyl. The sound of a car. Turning the flashlight off. Crouching down. A man stumbling and falling over him. A loud scream. The flashlight on. His own scream when he saw Mr. Hobson.

Betsy declared, "I don't know why I said that. Of course, he's not capable of such a thing. Do you have anything you'd like to say before I offer up my proposal?"

Still Betsy didn't sound angry, not even disappointed. Mydearie Mae was truly confused as to what was about to take place. She decided to let Betsy talk.

"Remember Lucinda, the blonde senior who used to slip out and smoke marijuana on the quadrangle at midnight and read poetry, or so we heard?" asked Betsy.

Mydearie Mae took her first sip of tea and nodded. Somehow their old breakfast duty rhythm was still there as Betsy talked and she listened.

"We were both on the judiciary committee at Hayden Harris when she was doing that, remember?"

Mydearie Mae could not imagine what this Lucinda had to do with her and Jimmy Clyde and Betsy. But the tea was starting to calm her. She nodded.

"I was the president, and it was your first year, of course. We had tried everything we knew to catch Lucinda but we never did. Remember how you and I stayed up until two that one morning? Remember what you said?"

Mydearie Mae looked up, uncertain.

"You said, 'I have an idea. In four hours we're going to have to cook breakfast. Let's just go to bed and forget Lucinda. Let her slip out if she wants to. What we don't know can't hurt us.'"

Betsy paused. She stared into her cup as if she were trying to read tea leaves.

"I thought about your advice for about ten seconds. I was sick and tired of losing sleep. I was being inconvenienced by the investigation more than Lucinda was. So what did it matter if she smoked a little pot and read poetry in the middle of the night?"

Betsy had her say and was waiting now for Mydearie Mae's response. She poured more tea.

"And this is why we're having lunch?" asked Mydearie Mae. "To talk about Lucinda and what I said?" Mydearie Mae tried not to sound confrontational.

"We're having lunch so that you will understand my position fully. I've been married to the same man for thirty years. Recently I learned of another life he'd had before I met him. In spite of that, I don't plan to divorce him. Ever. That would be inconvenient."

The waitress came over, but Betsy waved her away.

"He and I have had separate agendas for a long time now. He spends a lot of time in his workshop, and I'm very fond of my library work. But I like having a man in the house. And we especially enjoy Saturday mornings together, lazing around the table after a big breakfast, watching my spotless white sheets flap in the sunshine on the clothesline, smelling the Ginger Lilies he planted from the back yard, recalling Detroit and how we don't miss the snow—except for its silence."

Betsy said wistfully, "The snow silences everything, you know."

She paused, but only for a moment. "M.M, you can give up a part of a thing, without relinquishing it all. Know what I mean?" Betsy asked, reaching across to squeeze Mydearie Mae's hand. "Now, about their Ambrosia Chicken Salad. Ever had it? I know the Rosemary Flatbread is divine."

A toddler appeared in a navy outfit with a sailor collar and held up a French fry to Betsy. Just as Betsy was about to reach out to accept it, his mother whisked him away on her hip. Betsy's face darkened as she stared after them. Clearly her eyes were locked in a brown study.

When she turned back to Mydearie Mae, she muttered, "Those Saturdays I won't give up."

A Tale of Three Women

***

The rest of lunch was filled with small talk about college and various classmates; Betsy did most of the talking. Mydearie Mae picked at her chicken salad, too stunned to say much.

Mydearie Mae didn't yet fully understand the terms of this relationship Betsy was suggesting for the three of them—friendship and marriage and adultery. Betsy seemed to think they could simply link themselves tightly and neatly together, like a row of crochet stitches, chain stitched into a cluster.

In college, Betsy had crocheted an afghan with a pattern like that. She called it her bird's feet tracks. She snuggled up in it when they pulled an all-nighter studying for exams, but it was too nubby for Mydearie Mae. She preferred her plain cotton quilt.

Mydearie Mae had heard the story of a couple on the road between Brownville and Gordo whose livelihood was a country store just across the road from their home. That country store sold all the dry goods and food stuffs and gasoline and car parts that country stores necessarily sold. What was different about their country store was that it had a rather spacious bedroom conveniently built onto the back. There lived the young mistress of this man along with their two children. She worked with the man in the store. Mydearie Mae had often heard her mother fretting over this situation. Mydearie Mae's daddy would clear his throat and growl, "Something ought to be done about that harlot and those pitiful bastard children."

Mydearie Mae wondered what it was like for this mistress when the wife ran out of sugar or flour, or cornmeal. Would the mistress greet her cordially as if she were any other customer? Would the wife hold her head high and simply state her needs? If the children came in while the wife was there, how would the wife feel to see a child with her husband's eyes? Or his smile? What would it be like to bump into a neighbor there? Mydearie Mae considered this dilemma as she and Betsy embraced and promised to meet again soon for lunch.

Mydearie Mae's hands were trembling a little now as she unlocked the car door. She recalled what Jimmy Clyde had said about Betsy, how she crocheted one baby blanket after the other. Mydearie Mae supposed Betsy could probably do it blindfolded, with the same ease she used to put rollers in her hair without a mirror. She imagined Betsy's chest filled with pink and blue blankets that would soon take on the smell of cedar, instead of baby powder.

Epilogue

*T*he Community Building at the entrance is one of the few structures left standing in the little village of Brownville built by the Louisville investor, J. Graham Brown. Before the Brown Wood Preserving creosote plant opened in 1923, the tiny community was known as Red Valley, and all the houses were painted red. Not even the postmistress, who was acutely aware of the importance of names, could recite the history of an even earlier name for the village, Hog's Eye.

Creosote has not been able to preserve the houses from the rot of neglect and the raging of fires. The post office is no longer standing, nor is the doctor's office nearby. The commissary across the road is padlocked. It was on its porch that Mr. Brown's pet poodle, Woozems, whose ambition matched that of his owner's, had once yipped ferociously at Mr. Hobson's bloodhound as he ambled past. Just across the railroad tracks where the Smith house once stood, there is no evidence that a house was ever there. Sage grass and saw briars and pine saplings have reclaimed the lot. On up the road, the next house has gone up in one quick flame at the speed of a dried-out branch of cedar. The Quarters are no more.

The creosote plant is still in operation, but its output is limited. Very few poles of any kind lie on the pole yard. The little black steam engine is gone. No one here seems to remember just what happened to it. One man passing through with a camcorder said "Old 97" had been taken to Indiana Railroad Museum in French Lick, Indiana. French Lick lies about four hundred miles south of Detroit. The plant whistle still blows regularly, but the lives it governs are scant.

Gordo lies about twenty miles from Brownville, in Pickens County across the Sipsey River and through its swamp where Jimmy Clyde once hid out. To get there one has to pass by the Carrollton Court House, which has, according to Alabama's storyteller Kathryn Tucker Windham, and others, a man's face eerily etched by lightning into one of its courthouse windows and a lively story to go with it. Burned first by the Yankees, and rebuilt, the second courthouse was reputedly burned by Henry Wells. The face of Wells, falsely accused of arson, is the face etched permanently in a window of the courthouse and serves as a reminder of his ill-fated and wrongful death.

Some fifty miles east of the remains of Brownville is Birmingham, known as the Steel City.

Once it was renowned for its industry of steel making, but now its steel mills lie silent. At its tallest peak atop Red Mountain, the parts of a giant statue called the Iron Man, or Vulcan, lie rusting. It was conceived and cast from iron by an Italian sculptor for the publicity of the city at the World's Fair in St. Louis in 1904. Now there is a national campaign to restore Vulcan's 12,000 pounds of body parts, to have him whole again, so that he might rise up, fifty-six feet tall, overlooking the city with his torch.

Villages and cities change with time and distance. As do their residents.

About five miles south of the most prestigious shopping area in the city is a neighborhood called Greystone, a gated community that is immaculately landscaped. To enter, one must have a personal code. This keeps out all the riff-raff that might be selling encyclopedias or magazines door-to-door. A big gym sits just across the street. It is good to have a safe, posh place for people to exercise near home.

Mydearie Mae looks around the room of Nautilus equipment as she heads upstairs to the walking track. No sign of Miss Madeira. It has been two weeks since the day their name was called on the intercom at this gym, and they both responded to the summons. Mydearie Mae is still mulling over her odd relationship with Betsy and James, and this new knowledge of Miss Madeira and Jimmy Clyde's artistic tryst.

The mystery of the love letter gone awry has been solved: just as Madeira Mae had expected so long ago, the postmistress made a mistake. It was Miss Madeira who received Jimmy Clyde's love letter from Detroit. One tiny mistake had rippled like the surface of a creek hit by a gravel, and grown into great waves of confusion.

Mydearie Mae glances through the window of the aerobics room and tries to imagine where Jimmy Clyde and Betsy live in Gordo. Is he still practicing his art and, she, her crochet stitches? Does she herself want to know more about Jimmy Clyde's first grade teacher who posed nude as his watercolor model? And will she see her here at the gym? Will the two of them speak of Jimmy Clyde, or James C., when they meet again? Or will they just politely let that subject go, as a carver does his beloved wood, as he whittles, watching the wood separate into slivers, and the slivers sliding silently away?

Author's Afterword

On Fiction, Memory, and Roman à clef

Roman à clef. There now. We have taken the big key off the Big Word ring first: *a novel in which real people or events appear with invented names.* Literally, the phrase is translated, "novel with a key." *A Death in the Family* by James Agee is a good example.

That said, my intent here was not to write such a story. Nor did I intend to sift through the facts required of commentary, making more dry dust for critics to blow about over what is truth and what is a lie. What then did I intend to write?

Advice in my head came from many sources: Savannah writer and friend in the '90's, Arthur Gordon was adamant that "all great fiction is full of lies that tell the truth."

Alabama writer and close friend, Helen Norris, would tell me a decade later she was struck by a line of H.D.'s (Hilda Doolittle), "the finest of the Imagists," when someone asked her how she wrote her stories. Doolittle replied, "I do not write the story; the story writes me."

Helen cautioned me: "At some point in the story in which you are deeply involved, the story takes hold of you. It writes what it wants to write, what it needs. You are at the mercy of the tale."

I wanted to write, I thought, some stories peppered with people of a certain dignity—people who once lived where my family lived in a now defunct little company town called Brownville, twenty miles north of Tuscaloosa. We moved there in the summer of 1956, only a little better off than we had been as 'croppers, the same sharecroppers that Agee wrote about in 1941, along with photographer, Walker Evans. Their grand result was *Let Us Now Praise Famous Men*, although critics were not so convinced at first.

The unsettling scenes and people pictured in the Modern Classics version of that book are very familiar to me and my memories. The man in denim overalls on the cover could have been my daddy. I remember his determined stare, no doubt, in this case, at these dubious men traveling around Alabama taking pictures of ordinary barns, houses, and outhouses. Those eyes speak of an iron will to survive, even to prevail.

Not to launch a philosophical treatise on why or how I write here, but I will say memoir and fiction are so closely related for me, that as memory has it, I can barely tell them apart. I will simply use the case of the Jew's Harp and the Lane Cake to make my point. Before I ever read Harper Lee's *To Kill a Mockingbird*, my mama always baked a Lane Cake at Christmas that I'll bet could rival those of Lee's character, Miss Maudie Atkinson. Miss Maudie was the neighbor of the Finch family in the fictional town of Maycomb. Scout Finch, the narrator, allows that Miss Maudie "made the best cakes in the neighborhood" and was very generous in sharing them with Scout, Jem, and Dill. She made three little cakes for them every time she made a big cake.

According to the *Encyclopedia of Alabama*, the Lane Cake was a prize-winner first baked by Emma Rylander Lane of Clayton. It appeared in her self-published cookbook, *Some Good Things to Cook*, in 1898. Her directions called for the layers to be baked in pie pans lined with ungreased brown paper. *One wine glass of good whiskey or brandy* was to be added to the layers.

Still, I've found that few people I know have experienced the Lane Cake. And even fewer, a Jew's Harp. Like Scout's daddy, Atticus Finch, my daddy played a Jew's Harp, as well as a French Harp. A Jew's Harp is a small metal instrument held between the teeth and strummed with a forefinger while blowing onto it. The Lane Cake is more widely known than our meager family musical instruments.

Of the first folks I asked at One Nineteen Wellness Center in Birmingham, and at Publix, only Sarah, an Alabamian, had heard of and knew the Lane Cake well. Sarah doesn't bake the cake but her mother did, and Sarah still remembers how good it was. When I suggested to the exercise group that, because of the eight beaten egg whites required to be folded in, the layers might be dry, Sarah proclaimed "My mother's was *not* dry." Indeed the ideal sponge cake–one not using shortening–should be light, but some of my first efforts were more akin to rubber than to cloud.

Jo-Ann from Canada said that her family's traditional desserts for Christmas were not cakes, but pies–pumpkin and pecan. The grocery bagger who had retired here from Colorado to be near grandkids did not know the Lane Cake. He named the pecan pie as a favorite holiday dessert. Sue from New England said her family always had the Buche de Noel, or Yule log, a sheet cake baked, rolled up, unrolled and filled, rolled up again, and then decorated to look like a log.

My sister said that Mama's recipe for the Lane Cake came from Myrline Wicker in Brownville. The layers plus the filling made the tallest cake I'd ever seen. Mama gave Myrline's recipe to me after I was married, and I asked Mama about the one-fourth cup of bourbon suggested for the already generous filling of eight egg yolks, sugar, coconut, pecans, and raisins. Mama left the bourbon out. No question.

One Christmas season I baked two Lane Cakes. The first was for an early celebration with my two living sisters. Ree was quick to point out to me, and it was confirmed by Ann's daughter, Judy, too happily, it seemed to me, that the cake was not like Maw Smith's. *Hers always had four layers.* This is what happens when you think you know a recipe by heart. I checked the recipe when I got back home. Ree was right. It should have had four layers, not three. Mama's Lane Cake had no outside frosting— just the filling between the layers and on top. I announced outright that the white divinity frosting I used was one I had picked up several years ago from a recipe for coconut cake. They had no qualms about that addition.

For the actual Christmas Day gathering with my husband's family, I made the correction and cooked four layers and the eight-egg filling a few days before Christmas. On Christmas morning all that was left to complete the cake was cooking the fluffy divinity frosting and spreading it onto the sides and top. Then I added that essential flourish of green and red candied cherries.

I wondered if Myrline Wicker had used the bourbon in her cake, so I called her daughter, Marie, today. Marie thought her mother used the filling on the outside also as a frosting. On the question of bourbon, she was not certain. But she was clear on her mother's instructions about storing the cake in a cold room: the cake was not to be touched until Christmas Day.

When Aunt Alexandra comes to Maycomb to live with Atticus and the children, Scout says, "...Miss Maudie Atkinson baked a Lane Cake so loaded with shinny it made me tight."

I've tried adding a little "shinny" to my Lane Cake, but I can't tell that it improves the moistness or the taste of the cake. I was left with only a few sweet crumbs and memories.

Brownville was a town built in 1923 founded by James Graham Brown, the entrepreneur who also built the Brown Hotel in Louisville, KY, the official residence now of Spalding University's Master of Fine Arts in Writing program. Brown Wood Preserving Company and its creosote plant was the hub of the community. Its plant whistle governed the lives of the residents much like mission bells did the lives of its monks. Poles were preserved with creosote to be used for telephone and power lines. The plant is shut down and where the company houses once stood, nature has reclaimed her gardens. The spot where our house stood was across the railroad tracks and one house away from the Wicker house. There is no evidence of a commissary, or post office, or doctor's office, or school, or orchard, and no tennis courts–they were gone even when we lived there. Not even the grand two-story community building which functioned as both Methodist and Baptist churches on alternate

Sundays is left standing. Brownville is a place that could easily be as fictional as Harper Lee's town of Maycomb. Both, I remember, had the Lane Cake in common.

No matter what ingredient I might have added or omitted, I doubt that my Lane Cake, if stacked up against Myrline's, or Mama's, or Miss Maudie's, would have stood a gnat's chance for the blue ribbon. That's the power of memory and the use of both truth and lies in fiction. And a little mercy always helps.

An earlier version of part of this essay was published in WELD for Birmingham, editor, Glenny Brock.

Made in the USA
Columbia, SC
23 July 2020